F MONSTERS

'Chore-trex', 'The Book of Armaments' and 'The Forest for the Trees'
written by John Derevlany and Mark Hoffmeier

Produced by AMEET Sp. z o.o.
under license from the LEGO Group.

AMEET Sp. z o.o.
Nowe Sady 6, 94-102 Łódź
ameet@ameet.pl
www.ameet.pl

www.LEGO.com

LADYBIRD BOOKS
UK | USA | Canada | Ireland | Australia | India | New Zealand | South Africa
Ladybird Books is part of the Penguin Random House group of companies
whose addresses can be found at global.penguinrandomhouse.com.
www.penguin.co.uk www.puffin.co.uk www.ladybird.co.uk
Distributed by Penguin Books Ltd, 80 Strand, London, WC2R 0RL, UK
Please keep the Penguin Books Ltd address for future reference.
First published 2016

ISBN 978-0-241-27332-6
Printed in Poland – 001

Item name: LEGO® NEXO KNIGHTS™. Swarm of Monsters
Series: LNR
Item number: LNR-802
Batch: 01/GB

SWARM OF MONSTERS

CONTENTS

FORTREX, SWEET FORTREX!

CLAY

The Fortrex has a training room where you can practise to your heart's content, plus a special collector's edition of the Knight's Code.

MACY

There's a wonderful armoury, worthy of princesses who prefer fighting battles to being entertained by minstrels!

MERLOK 2.0

The Fortrex is also the headquarters of a cybernetic wizard who supplies the Knights with NEXO Powers by uploading them to their shields – that's me!

When a kingdom is in danger, it's up to the knights to defend the realm. But these Knights aren't your average chivalrous strangers... they're the LEGO® NEXO KNIGHTS™ heroes! These Knights use digital magic and travel in style in the Fortrex, the most well-defended mobile fortress ever! The Fortrex contains everything a knight could ever dream of. Take a look for yourself!

THAT'S JUST HOW THE STORIES GO

When a kingdom is thriving and living happily ever after, there's usually someone just waiting to destroy it all! And in some cases, two people! When one of them has a magical army and the other has an evil guard on wheels, who knows what will happen?

Jestro feels like a powerful and evil ruler behind the wheel of his Evil Mobile . . . at least until the NEXO KNIGHTS heroes arrive to drive him away!

The Book of Monsters doesn't just feel like a powerful and evil ruler – he *is* the powerful and evil ruler of all the monsters within his pages.

CHORE-TREX

'It smells kinda funny,' said Lance Richmond, covering his face with his hands. 'Richmonds always smell like honey and lilacs.'

Clay stopped oiling his vehicle in the NEXO KNIGHTS Vehicle Maintenance Bay. 'Yes, a rubbish receptacle can sometimes smell like, wait for it . . . rubbish,' said Clay. 'That's why I need you to take it outside to the dump.'

Lance stared at the bin for a moment, then turned to protest again. 'Did I mention that I might get smelly if I touch it?'

Frustrated, Clay tried to speak calmly, 'You said you were available to help me with chores today. Taking out the bin is a pretty basic chore, whether you feel like it or not.'

'I just don't want to smell like it,' Lance sighed, quickly tying up the rubbish bag and running outside.

Three seconds later, he sprinted back in. 'When I said I'd help, I had no idea that I was required to do soooo many things.'

Clay shook his head. 'You've been helping for less than five minutes, Lance.'

'So . . . we're done?' Lance replied hopefully.

'Negative,' replied Clay.

'Why do *I* have to do this kind of thing? Don't we have squirebots to do this stuff? I mean . . . that's why they're . . . squirebots, right?'

Clay shook his head again, and began tossing the oily rags he'd been using into the bin.

'I just emptied that and now you're filling it up again,' protested Lance. 'Chores are no fun.'

'Chores build character,' said Clay, going back to his maintenance. 'Your Mecha Horse needs an overhaul. Why don't you start on that?'

Lance shuffled over to his Mecha Horse. 'Character? I'm a Richmond. I can *buy* all the character I need.' He bent down and pretended to inspect his Mecha Horse.

Finished with his vehicle, Clay came over to check on Lance's progress. 'I laminated this fifty-seven-point Mecha Horse inspection checklist for you,' he said, handing the long list to Lance. 'You'll notice that "make mirrors sparkle" is included in item numbers twenty-one, thirty-nine and fifty-seven.' Clay smiled slyly. 'I know how much you like to look at your spotless reflection. What do you think?'

Lance's heart sunk as he looked through the list . . . and that was before he noticed there was a page two.

'Oh boy . . . another whole page of chores,' said Lance, giving Clay a sarcastic thumbs up.

'Great,' Clay replied. 'I'm off to flush the converters. I'll be back to check on you in a while.'

And off Clay strolled out of the Vehicle Maintenance Bay, leaving Lance sulking behind him.

'Number one: Clean hover-drive particle filter,' Lance read with a groan. 'BORING! I'm way too busy being adored by the masses to do all of this.'

Lance decided to go to his parents' house where there would be a dozen squirebot servants to do all fifty-seven items on the checklist. He hopped on his Mecha Horse and pulled out of the bay.

This is much more fun than hanging with Clay and doing his chores, Lance thought, tearing through the country roads.

He leaned into a particularly tight turn and heard a loud *BA-THUMP . . . flapapapap*! His Mecha Horse suddenly tipped nose-down and dived towards the road, not stopping until it crashed into a large tree.

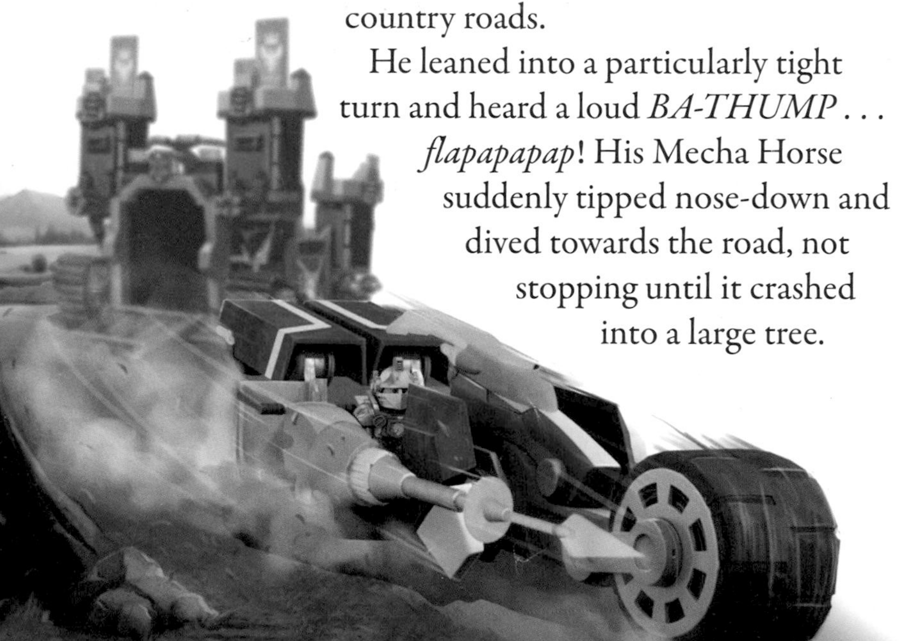

Lance hopped off the Mecha Horse and checked for any sign of injury. 'Thank goodness I'm okay,' he said, carefully checking that he was in one piece. 'Not a hair out of place.'

Lance turned his attention to the broken Mecha Horse, giving it a once-over. 'What happened to you?' He tried to get its engine going again, but it just sputtered and smoked.

Giving up, Lance pulled out his phone and dialled. 'Hey, Dad. Yeah, I was coming to see you but the Mecha Horse fizzled out on me. Can you please send some squirebots to come and get me?'

Half an hour later, Lance was getting a bad feeling about being alone in the deserted countryside. Where were the squirebots?

Just then, Jestro and the Book of Monsters popped out of the forest next to the road and stared at the stranded Lance.

'Anyone need a *toad*?' Jestro asked, as he waved his wand over the Book of Monsters. *Puff!* Out of the Book of Monsters' mouth hopped a very ordinary toad.

'A toad?' the Book of Monsters scoffed. 'I said, "We'll surprise him" and you were supposed to say, "Anyone need a tow?" as we jumped out at him.'

‘I got it. But I didn’t want to help him,’ whined Jestro.

‘We aren’t gonna help him, you purple-and-red wearing goof!’ replied the Book. ‘We’re gonna *capture* him!’

‘Oh, good idea!’ cried Jestro. He waved his wand over the Book of Monsters again and brought forth a slew of Globlins.

‘Great – chores, a broken Mecha Horse and now monsters,’ said Lance, preparing for battle. He pulled out his lance and lunged forward at a couple of Globlins. *SMACK! SMACK!* Then he spun round and smacked a Globlin behind him.

'You're so fancy when you fight,' the Book of Monsters remarked. 'But you really should look up occasionally.'

A Bloblin launched itself from a nearby tree. A large woven parachute opened up behind it and it floated lazily down.

Lance chuckled, 'You'll need to be faster than that to surprise me.'

Just then, Burnzie sprang towards Lance's weapon, knocking it away from him as the parachuting Bloblin landed on the Knight. It wrapped the unarmed Lance in the woven parachute.

‘Yes! We nabbed ourselves a Knight!’ cheered Jestro, as Burnzie threw Lance over his shoulder in the parachute bag.

‘I’m not sure this one’s in the bag just yet!’ announced Clay, pulling up in his very shiny Rumble Blade.

‘But he is,’ said the Book of Monsters. ‘Literally . . . in the bag. There he is.’

‘Not for long,’ Clay yelled, as he skidded to a stop and leaped out of his vehicle. He raised his shield. ‘NEXOOOO KNIGHTS!’

‘NEXO Power –’ said Merlok 2.0, his swirl of digi-magic forming in the sky above Clay’s shield – ‘Moth Swarm!’

A digi-magic Moth Swarm formed over Clay’s shield and downloaded, powering up his sword. Clay leaped into the air and somersaulted towards Burnzie. Then he pointed his sword towards Lance and shot the magical Moth Swarm at the bag. A giant moth flew towards it, trailing sparkling dust everywhere and quickly devoured the bag.

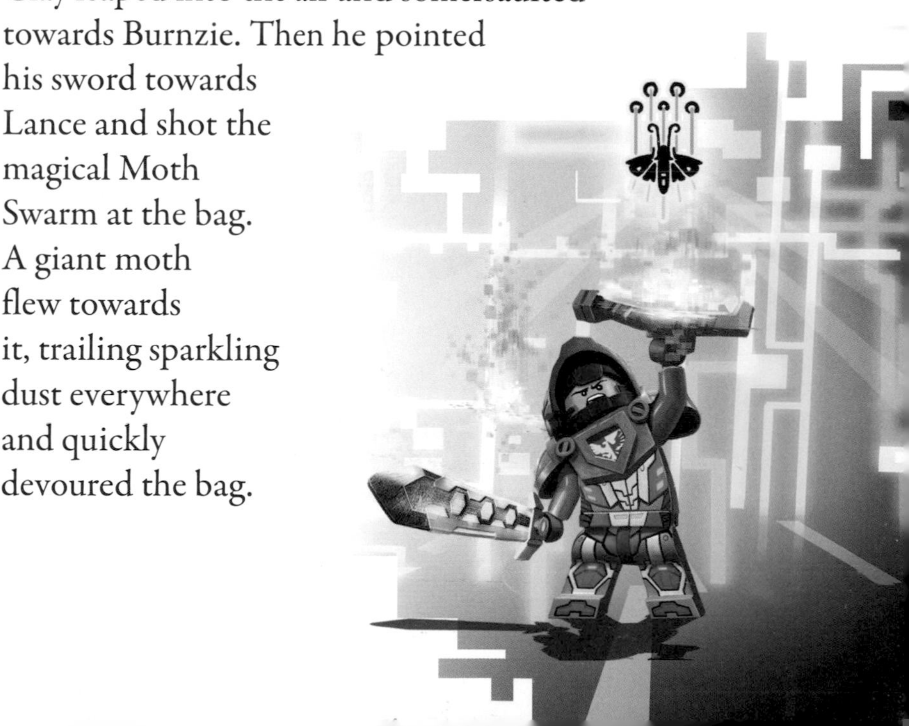

Freed, Lance began to hop about. 'Bugs,' he cried nervously. 'Why'd it have to be bugs?'

'I hate those NOTHING Knights and their NEXO Powers,' wailed the Book of Monsters as he and Jestro hurried quickly back into the forest.

'I know!' complained Jestro. 'It's such a *chore* trying to beat them!'

'That Moorington guy is the worst,' said the Book. 'Always so organized and prepared. Makes me wanna barf up a monst– . . . but not right now. I've got a bit of a dodgy stomach.'

Later, back at the Vehicle Maintenance Bay, Clay slid out from under Lance's Mecha Horse and said, 'Laaance.'

'Still combing the magic dust out of my hair,' Lance replied, though he was really just spending some 'me time' in front of the mirror.

'I had a look at the engine,' said Clay. 'I think it failed because of this dirty filter.'

'I'd say that would be highly likely,' agreed Lance. 'I noticed how dirty it was before I took the Mecha Horse out.'

Clay crossed his arms and gave Lance a look.

'I know. I know. If I'd done my chores, my Mecha Horse wouldn't have broken down.'

'It's not just that, Lance,' said Clay. 'You need to take proper care of *all* your things, and then they can take care of you.'

'Okay, I get it,' Lance admitted. 'Chores . . . are . . . important.'

'I'm glad you're finally coming round, Lance,' Clay said proudly. 'Thanks to my constant vigilance, *my* vehicles are in tip-top shape.'

'And I appreciate that,' said Lance. 'Speaking of which . . . can I borrow your Rumble Blade to go to my movie premiere tonight?'

THE BOOK OF ARMAMENTS

'My team is going to beat yours,' Clay taunted Aaron. 'And it will all be down to my superior researching skills.'

The Knights were on their way to the Academy library to research their Fantasy Joust teams.

As Aaron entered, he bumped into a girl leaving the library in a hurry. Several of her books went flying, and Aaron was knocked to the ground.

'Excuse my friend, fair maiden,' said Clay, turning on his charm. 'We'll gather your books for you.'

'No thanks,' the girl replied, clutching a single book. 'Gotta go.'

'Hey!' Aaron called after her. 'You forgot all these books!'

'I've got the one I want, thanks,' shouted the girl, as she vanished from sight.

Aaron picked up the books, puzzled. 'Who checks out a dozen books and abandons eleven?' He started through the library doors when – *BLAM*! Persnickety Marge came whizzing out of the library, crashed into Aaron and knocked him to the ground again.

Persnickety Marge yelled, 'That girl just stole a book from the Magic Non-fiction section!'

'She stole a book from a library where you can check out books for free?' Clay asked. 'You're kidding.'

Persnickety Marge looked seriously at Clay. 'I never kid about non-fiction. Fiction . . . now that's another story.'

Aaron chuckled. 'Another story, HA! Library humour.'

Clay continued, 'What book did she steal?'

'The *Book of Armaments*!' said Principal Brickland as he joined them. He wasn't pleased. 'And I know who took it.'

Brickland pulled up the library's security-camera footage on a tablet. 'Here is Lavaria walking into the library's periodical section in disguise. Clay, Aaron, I need you to track down that book.'

‘We’ll get started straight away,’ Clay said, taking charge of the situation. ‘We won’t let you down!’

The Book of Monsters and Jestro waited by the village of Bucketon’s ‘World’s Largest Bucket’.

‘I don’t know about this,’ said Jestro as his knees knocked together nervously. ‘Lavaria said she’d be here by now. Maybe something happened to her? Maybe the Knights found her and set a trap for us?’

‘Yeesh, stop quaking in your oversized hat, joke-boy,’ retorted the Book of Monsters. ‘Lavaria is a master of disguise. Uh, mistress of disguise. Whatever. For all we know, she may already be here.’

Just then, someone whispered to Jestro, ‘You can’t see me? It’s because I’m looking a little pale.’

'Who said that?' asked Jestro, panicked. Jestro whipped his head around but couldn't see anything other than the giant bucket.

Lavaria stepped out of her hiding place, right next to the bucket. 'It's me, boss-man. Relax.'

'Oooh, a little *pail* – I get it. Camouflaged to look like you're part of the bucket,' said Jestro, always pleased by Lavaria's stealthiness. 'Hide again. I want to find you. I've read all the *Find the knight in the striped shirt* books!'

'Like we've got time for that!' said the Book of Monsters impatiently. Just feed me the *Book of Armaments* and let's get looting!'

'Hello. Hellllοooo. Hellllllοooooo!' Aaron cried as he came flying around the giant bucket. 'Man, the acoustics are *awesome* near this big bucket. We gotta book it for Axl's band and really rock it.'

'Gah! The Knights! Eat it, Book, EAT IT!' Jestro quickly shoved the *Book of Armaments* into the Book of Monsters' mouth.

The Book of Monsters swallowed the *Book of Armaments* and burped up a cloud of purple smoke. 'Eh, give a guy a little warning before you jam pages down his throat!' said the Book of Monsters, as he started shaking and puffing up, 'I'm gonna need some antacid here . . . *BURRRRRP*!'

Jestro quickly threw open the Book of Monsters and waved his staff over the pages.

‘Swords and bows and lots of maces,’ chanted Jestro. ‘C’mon out and smash these places!’

A stream of monsters and armaments gushed from the Book. The various monsters were armed with swords, maces, lances, pikes, halberds, axes and warhammers! They looked *very* menacing!

Clay grabbed Aaron and pulled him into a nearby doorway. 'We need a plan of attack.'

Hordes of monsters shook their weapons and rushed at the Knights. Aaron and Clay marvelled at the variety of weaponry carried by the crazy Lava Monster.

Quick-thinking Clay ordered Aaron into the air on his hover shield. 'You take 'em on from the sky, I'll take 'em down from the ground.'

'Right, Clay-man,' said Aaron as he let loose with a few electronic bolts, knocking back some charging monsters.

Clay moved in on the ground and knocked back several monsters with some amazing sword work. 'There are way too many monsters to fight . . . and this time they're all armed!'

‘Too many?’ Jestro jested in his usual nasally tone. ‘Nah, I want MORE monsters!’

More monsters came out of the Book. Moltor materialized. He grunted and slammed his oversized fist into the bucket, making a fairly large dent.

Aaron flew by and shot electric bolts at Moltor. ‘Hey, no fair attacking a poor helpless bucket.’

Clay, surrounded by monsters wielding maces, blocked their blows. 'You guys need to be more careful with your dangerous toys.'

The mace-swinging monsters closed in and were nearly on top of Clay. He jumped into the air, flipped and grabbed Aaron's hand as he flew by on his hover shield. The maces, still swinging, got a bit too close to each other and the monsters knocked each other out!

'Cool moves, Clay-man!' said Aaron excitedly.

Aaron set Clay down, 'That was close. How about you call down a little extra help?'

'Totally agree with your thinking, Aaron,' said Clay, raising his shield. He called out over his comm-link to the Fortrex. 'NEXOOOO KNIGHTS!'

'NEXO Power –' said Merlok 2.0 as his swirl of digi-magic pixels formed in the sky above Clay's shield – 'Whirlwind!'

Above Clay's shield an awesome digi-magic whirlwind formed. Then, with a *WHOOSH*, it downloaded the power to Clay's shield, powering up both Clay and Aaron's weapons and armour. They were ready to rock!

'Oooo, I hate their special powers!' cried the Book of Monsters as Clay and Aaron used their weapons.

Upon reaching the monsters, the Whirlwind Power confused them greatly, making them easy pickings for Clay and Aaron.

'No fair! No fair!' yelled the Book of Monsters as monsters streamed back into his mouth.

Finally, when all the monsters were dispatched and the weapons collected, the Book of Monsters belched up the *Book of Armaments*, which shot out of his mouth and over to Aaron.

'I'll take that,' said Aaron, from his hover shield. 'Yikes, what's that smell?'

'I never brush my teeth,' said the Book of Monsters. 'I think it's all part of my charm.' He turned to Jestro, 'I also think it's time to skedaddle!'

The Book of Monsters and Jestro quickly retreated.

The next morning, Aaron and Clay triumphantly handed Persnickety Marge the *Book of Armaments*.

'We are proud and honoured to be the ones to return this to you,' said Clay.

Persnickety Marge took the book, smiled and scanned it. 'I'll put you back where you belong in a little bit,' she whispered to it, placing it down gently on the returns shelf. Then she turned to the Knights, 'Now, the money –'

'No, no,' said Clay in his most heroic voice. 'There's no need for a reward. Seeing that smile on your face is enough reward for us.'

'Reward?' countered Persnickety Marge, 'No. This book's overdue. So . . . PAY UP!'

THE FOREST FOR THE TREES

'Oh, I can't wait . . . I – CAN'T – WAIT!' cried Axl happily, as he ran down the open drawbridge of the Fortrex.

'Axl, please wait!' cried Chef Éclair, scurrying down the ramp behind the big NEXO KNIGHTS hero. 'My little legs can't move as swiftly as yours. I am but a humble, gourmet chef-bot.'

'Come on! I've been looking forward to this ever since you told me that our travels through Knighton would take us near the Dark Woods so we could hunt for –' Axl paused and smiled – 'miggleberries!'

Chef Éclair had been serving a delicious lunch in the Fortrex's command centre when he'd seen on the map that they would be travelling near the Dark Woods. It was the only place in the kingdom the elusive miggleberry could be found.

'Let's kick it into high gear,' cried Axl as he scooped up the slow-moving Chef Éclair. 'We've got to get berry hunting!'

Axl moved into the Dark Woods with visions of juicy, succulent berries dancing in his head.

'I HATE this dark forest,' said Jestro, tripping over a root as he tried to keep up with the Bookkeeper, who was carrying the Book of Monsters.

'Stop your whining,' said the Book of Monsters. 'We're lookin' to add to my collection of forest fiends.'

Sniffing something out, the Book of Monsters pointed the Bookkeeper down a narrow path. 'No, not that way!' cried the Book. 'The other way! Go the *other* way!'

Meanwhile, in another part of the forest, Axl tiptoed behind Chef Éclair as the squirebot used his gastronomic sensors to sniff out miggleberries.

'Well? Is there something here?'

'Uhhhhhh, no,' responded Chef Éclair, sniffing around the roots of a big tree. 'But, I think there is something this way . . .'

Chef Éclair led Axl down a path to the centre of the forest, towards the tallest tree. As they headed there, Axl thought he heard something and looked around.

Nothing! But when he turned back to the path, Chef Éclair was gone! He'd followed his squirebot sensors off into the forest, tracking miggleberries.

'Chef! Chef?' cried Axl looking round again.

Chef Éclair had wandered off the path and into the darkness. He sniffed and sniffed until . . . *BONK*! He ran right into the trunk of the tallest tree in the forest.

'Axl, I think we are getting close,' said Chef Éclair. 'Axl?' The chef turned around to see that Axl wasn't behind him.

Then suddenly, his sensitive sensors spun him around and pulled his face straight down near the roots of a big tree.

'Can it be true? I'm detecting ripe miggleberries!' said the chef excitedly.

'Look, it's that little chef-bot from the Fortrex,' said Jestro, peering through some undergrowth. The Bookkeeper came up beside him, pointing the Book of Monsters through the branches so he could see Chef Éclair under the tall tree, nose down looking for berries.

'Perfect!' said the Book of Monsters. 'If we grab him we can find out all about the inner workings of the Fortrex!'

'Well, at least the inner workings of the Fortrex kitchen,' replied Jestro.

'Look, clown-boy, don't throw cold gravy on my plan. We grab the chef and then we've got bargaining power. Open me to your "Forest Monsters" chapter. There are some talented Tree Monsters in there.'

The Bookkeeper dropped the Book of Monsters down and Jestro quickly *leafed* through his pages.

'Aha!' said Jestro as he waved his staff over the book. 'Leafy, leafy monsters, be the opposite of good; come out of this book and attack in the Dark Woods!'

FLASH! POOF! ZAP! The Forest Monsters popped out of the Book in a cloud of magical sparks. Jestro smiled and laughed. He loved having monsters to do his evil bidding and directed the leafy villains straight towards Chef Éclair, who was still rummaging through the berry bushes around the giant tree.

Suddenly, the excited chef found his prize – miggleberries!

'*Magnifique!*' cried the chef.

But, as he did so, the dirt at his feet stirred, and to his horror, the Mushlord Marauder climbed out of the ground!

The Mushlord Marauder shook his powerful sword, Fungaliber, at the chef. 'Put those down!'

Chef Éclair turned and ran, right into the waiting arms of Axl!

'Chef, where ya been?!' said Axl. 'This forest is fillin' up with monsters!'

WHAM! A tree next to them was split in two by the powerful club of the Tree Monster Deadwood and his ever-present companion, Knot.

'Make kindling out of 'em, Deadwood!' cried Knot as the mighty monster swung his heavy, wooden club again.

Axl quickly grabbed Chef Éclair, ducked another blow from Deadwood, then shouldered his way past the Mushlord Marauder, who was coming up from behind.

With Chef Éclair tucked under one arm, Axl bounded down the path in the woods, using his axe to cut up the undergrowth. As they raced towards a clearing, a bush rose up in front of them! It was Bramblina!

'Shrub-a-dub-dub!' she cried as she snapped her razor-sharp thorn whips at them.

'*Aidez-moi!*' said Chef Éclair. 'We have been ambushed by a . . . bush!'

Axl swung his powerful axe at Bramblina, but she dodged it and cracked her whips.

'How about some Sour Berry Globlins?' said Bramblina, making Globlins appear. The Globlins spat exploding seeds around Axl and Chef Éclair, backing them into the clearing where the Mushlord Marauder, Deadwood and Knot were all moving in from behind to trap them!

The terrifying Tree Monsters surrounded Axl and Chef Éclair, as Jestro and the Book of Monsters peeked out from behind a nearby bush.

'They're so surrounded it's silly,' said Jestro, giddy with excitement. Jestro turned – as did everyone in the clearing – when they heard the *THUD-THUD-THUD* of giant footsteps. It was . . . the huge Elm of the Dark Realm!

'You dare disturb my woods? Now you will PAY!' shouted the thundering Tree Monster, ready to pounce.

'*Quelle horreur!*' exclaimed Chef Éclair. 'We must make like a tree . . . and leave!'

'I've got a better idea,' said Axl, getting on his comm-link to the Fortrex. 'Merlok, I need a NEXO Power, quick!'

The wicked monsters moved in closer to Axl and Chef Éclair as Axl tried to hold them off with his axe. Bramblina cracked her thorny whips, Deadwood swung his massive club and the Mushlord Marauder released a Storm of Spores in Axl and Chef Éclair's direction.

Things were looking very grim for Axl and Éclair. But then Axl's comm-link crackled. It was Merlok.

'Just had to find the perfect power for you. Prepare for the scan!'

''Bout time,' said Axl, raising his shield. 'NEXOOOO KNIGHTS!'

'NEXO Power–' said Merlok 2.0, as his swirl of digi-magic pixels formed in the sky above Axl – 'Fire Tornado!'

The pixels in the digi-magic signal burst to life, swirled into the fiery, glowing orange symbol of a tornado, then downloaded to Axl's shield with a *whoosh*! The Knight turned his glowing axe towards his foresty foes, who trembled in fear at his fiery, tornado-powered axe.

'I hate those NEXO Powers!' said Bramblina.

‘Oh boy,’ said the Book of Monsters, watching. ‘I think we’re in trouble.’

Axl used his NEXO Power to lay into the Tree Monsters, and with quick strikes of his axe, magically dispatched all the monsters back into the Book of Monsters.

Then, Axl turned and faced off with his final foe, The Elm of the Dark Realm.

'Leaf us alone!' cried Axl, spinning himself round like a fiery tornado and chopping at the mighty tree. It flashed as its magic was undone and its monstery essence was also sent back into the Book of Monsters.

Having been defeated, Jestro and the Book of Monsters quickly ran out of the woods, afraid that Axl was going to turn his NEXO Power towards them!

Axl picked up Chef Éclair and looked at him. 'All this trouble to get fresh miggleberries,' said Axl. 'Was it worth it, Chef?'

'*You* will have to be the judge of that,' said Éclair, showing Axl the berries he had kept safe during the battle.

Back in the safety of the Fortrex's kitchen, Chef Éclair pulled the freshly baked miggleberry tart out of the oven and presented it to Axl.

Axl took a bite, savoured it, then smiled broadly. '*Totally* worth it!'

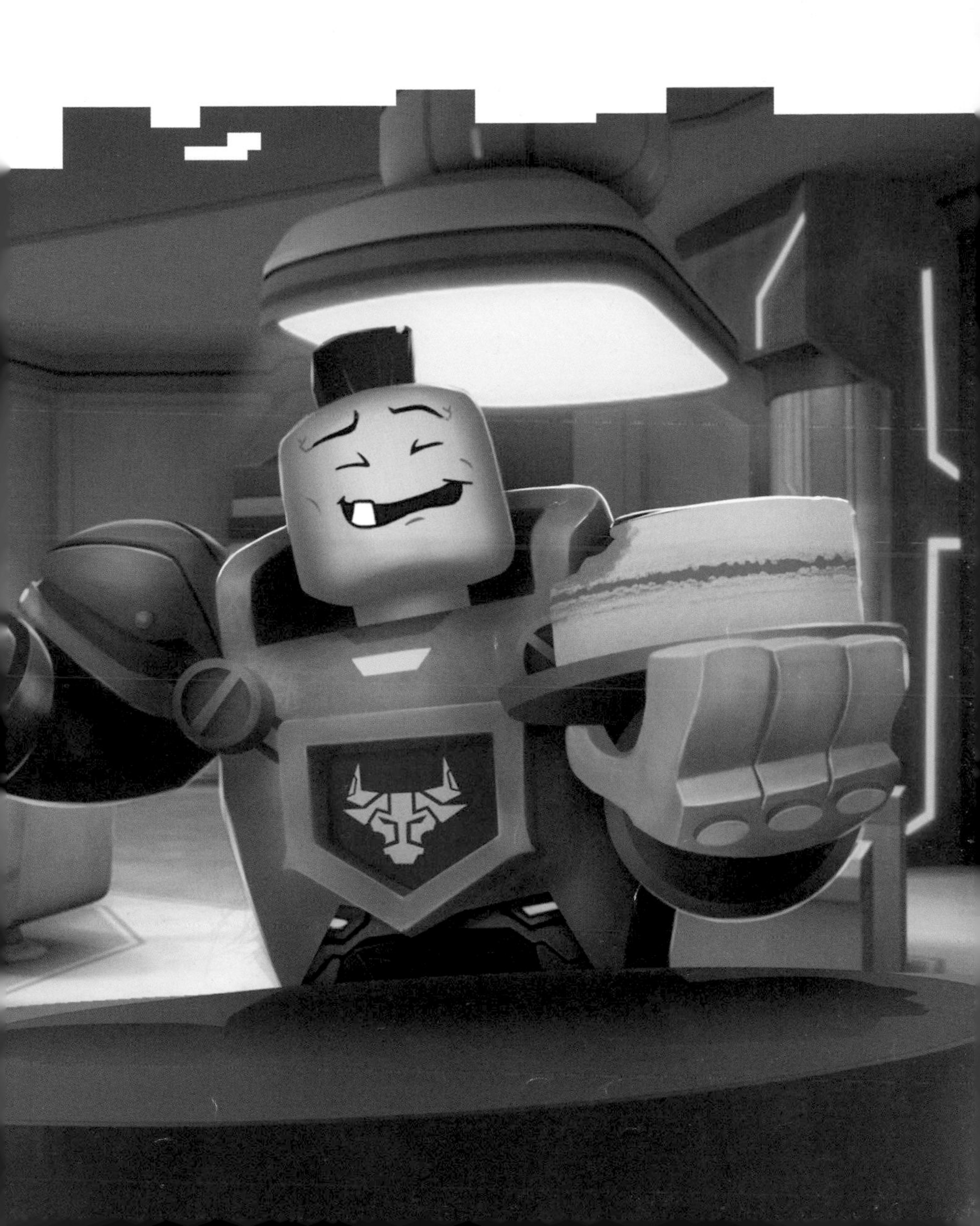

FOREST MONSTERS

As dangerous as Lava Monsters, but built from plants and mushrooms... very bad and very organic!

GLOSSARY

BRAMBLINA
She's a thorny Forest Monster with a beautiful name and very malicious barbed creepers! Bramblina and her Sour Berry Globlins love to set traps for the villagers. They like spitting out exploding seeds and staining clothes permanently with their juice!

BUCKETON
A town in Knighton that is famous for being the home of the World's Largest Bucket! Well . . . every town likes to be famous for something!

CHEF ÉCLAIR
This royal squirebot master-chef is appreciated most by Axl, whom he teaches to cook. The Chef does two things best – cooking and screaming at Axl when he ruins his soufflés.

DARK WOODS

This magical place is absolutely perilous, unless you're friends with the Forest Monsters. Otherwise, only go there if you want to experience the feeling of submerging your soul neck-deep in nettles.

DEADWOOD AND KNOT

His name's Deadwood, because all his leaves died ages ago . . . along with most of his brain cells. Luckily, he's got a knot on his belt (called Knot) to do all his thinking for him. They're not exactly a dynamic duo, but if you need to put the 'Fear of the Forest' in your foes, these two will beat anyone in their path to a pulp – a *wood* pulp that is.

FIRE TORNADO

One of the great forces of digital magic. It summons a fiery tornado that burns everything in its path.

MOTH SWARM

Another great force of digital magic. A giant moth moves from one side to the other, leaving sparkling dust behind and making all enemies vulnerable to an attack.

PERSNICKETY MARGE

A librarian working at the Royal Academy library. She's just like any other squirebot librarian – well-read, methodical, old fashioned and a bit grumpy.

PRINCIPAL BRICKLAND

A teacher at the Royal Academy. He's the oldest professor there – he even remembers Merlok's grandfather and the days when knights rode actual horses!

ROYAL ACADEMY

A school where Knights are trained to defend the borders and keep order in Knighton. It hasn't had that many students and recently only five of them graduated. Fortunately, Clay, Axl, Macy, Lance, and Aaron have a full magic arsenal at their disposal.

THE ELM OF THE DARK REALM

This Tree Monster has some serious issues. He is out for revenge, ruthlessly devouring the bodies and souls of anyone who has ever misused a piece of timber, or even got a splinter! So if you value your life, stay away from anything made of wood – that includes toothpicks and paper products.

THE MUSHLORD MARAUDER

This one is one hundred per cent all-natural, gluten-free EVIL. He carries a huge sword called Fungalibur, which he likes to use often. He also likes to use a Storm of Spores that turn into man-eating mushrooms and besiege everyone. Yeesh . . . let's move on quickly . . .

WHIRLWIND

One of the great forces of digital magic. Its strike pushes the enemies into the centre of a vicious tornado.